Getting Lost:
The Creek

Samantha Patterson

ISBN 978-1-957262-72-7 (Paperback)
978-1-957262-79-6 (Hardback)

Getting Lost: The Creek

Copyright © 2023 by Samantha Patterson.

Yorkshire Publishing
1425 E 41st Pl
Tulsa, OK 74105
www.YorkshirePublishing.com
918.394.2665

Printed in the USA

For my Dad, hope I made you proud!

Papaw and Nana, up bright and early,
listening to the rooster crowing.
Oh, how fast these boys are growing!

Loaded in the buggy with
lunch in the back.
A new adventure, they won't lack.

Down the path and through the trees,
Listening to the sounds of
the buzzing bees.
Little boys on hands and knees.

Digging, searching, picking up rocks.
Feet in the water without any socks.

Across the water they throw
stones, smooth and flat.
Some go "Kur-plunk".
Some go "Kur-splat".

Papaw takes time to show each one how.
One, two, three...those pebbles
are skipping now.

Eason cries out, "Hey, look at me,"
Climbing on a log, wanting
the others to see.

Archer begins walking up
the old bent tree.
David is following, "Wait up for me!"

Kenny takes off,
He's looking for his favorite wildlife.

Splashing and playing with
much to discover,
Tiny fish swimming quickly for cover.

The sun above is warm and bright,
Dragonflies are taking flight.

Muddy water between their toes,
Who knows where the afternoon goes?

The summer sun starts to fade,
Little boys rest in the shade.

Back up the path, out through the trees,
Listening to the buzzing bees,
Little boys on their knees.

What started as the adventures of four,
has grown into so much more.

At the end of the trail, cousins
and friends all gather round.
Laughing, playing, making
little boy sounds.

Crackers in hand,
marshmallows on wires.
Warming faces, hands, and
hearts by the fire.
Fun was had, memories made,
In the sun and in the shade.

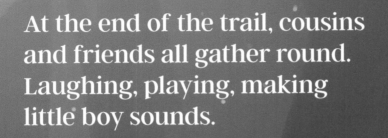

Stories are told, the moon starts to glow.
Songs are sung, soft and low.

Eyes grow heavy, the world slows.
Stars twinkle, the fire still glows.

One by one, they head to the tent.
Tired, but happy with how the day went.

Little boys all tucked in....
Waiting to Get Lost again!

Ingram Content Group UK Ltd.
Milton Keynes UK
UKHW050642070323
418149UK00002B/103